TURK AND RUNT

Story by Lisa Wheeler ✦ Pictures by Frank Ansley

SCHOLASTIC INC.

New York Toronto London Auckland Sydney
Mexico City New Delhi Hong Kong Buenos Aires

ISBN 0-439-59272-0

12 11 10 9 8 7 6 5 4 3 2 1   4 5 6 7 8/0

Printed in the U.S.A.   24

First Scholastic printing, November 2003

Book design and display typeface by Frank Ansley

The text of this book is set in AG Book Rounded and the display type is set in Ansley Bold.

The illustrations are rendered in ink and watercolor.

For Dick and Steve, my two favorite turkeys. Gobble, gobble!
—L. W.

For Brennan, our new grandtot, and for Denys, who knows
from turkeys.
—F. A.

Turk's parents were so proud of him.

He was the biggest, strongest, and most graceful bird on Wishbone Farm.

"He's a dancer," said his mother.

"He's an athlete," said his father.

"He's a goner," said his brother, Runt.

But no one ever listened to Runt.

Every year, the farm animals looked forward
to the excitement of autumn.

Carloads of people came to pick red, ripe apples
from the orchard in September.

Folks arrived to choose plump, orange pumpkins
from the field in October.

And come November, it was turkey time.

One by one, the fattest, roundest turkeys were chosen.

"Chosen for what?" asked Turk.

"To be the lead dancer in *Swan Lake*," said his mother.

"To play in the Thanksgiving Day football game," said his father.

"To be roasted and gently basted," said his brother, Runt.

But no one ever listened to Runt.

So every morning in November, the family watched Turk
practice his dance steps.

"One . . . two . . . three . . . lift!"

And every afternoon, the family watched Turk
practice his football moves.

"Sixteen, twenty-three, forty-seven . . . hike!"

"He's getting stronger," said his mother.

"He's getting bigger," said his father.

"He's getting juicier," said Runt.

Two days before Thanksgiving, Madame Waddelle, the famous ballet instructor, arrived at Wishbone Farm. She came to choose a turkey.

"An audition!" Mother squealed. "It's your time to shine.

Go out there and shake those tail feathers!"

Turk gracefully danced to the front of the barnyard.

He leaped.

He spun.

He twirled and whirled.

He did a triple somersault and landed in a split!

"Look at zee size of zose drumsticks!" said Madame Waddelle.

"Zat is a beautiful bird!"

Mother beamed.

Father puffed out his feathers with pride.

Runt puffed out his feathers too.

Then he threw himself on the ground.

He flapped.

He flopped.

He hissed and sputtered.

He gobbled like a maniac as
he chased Madame Waddelle
out of the barnyard.
"Sacre bleu!" screamed Madame
Waddelle. "Zees birds are crazy!"

Then she drove far, far away
from Wishbone Farm.

"No *Swan Lake!*" cried Mother.
"No starring role!" cried Father.
"No roasted Turk with chestnut dressing!"
  cried Runt. "Hooray!"

But no one ever listened to Runt.

The day before Thanksgiving, Coach Giblet of the Crow City Corn Shuckers came to pick out a turkey.

"This is your big chance," said Father. "Get out there and strut your stuff!"

Turk sprinted to the front of the barnyard.

He bobbed. He weaved.

He tackled and dived.

He mowed down every turkey who got in his way.

"That's one healthy-looking bird!" said Coach Giblet.

"Only the biggest and the best for my team."

Father grinned proudly.

Mother got tears in her eyes.

Runt got tears in his eyes too.
Then his beak began to drip.

He coughed. He wheezed.

He sniffled and sneezed.

He fell to the ground in a hacking fit
of quivering feathers.

"Good gravy!" shouted the coach as he hopped back onto the team bus.

"These are very sick birds. The Corn Shuckers deserve better."

Then he sped far, far away from Wishbone Farm.

"No football contract!" cried Father.

"No TV commercials!" cried Mother.

"No Turk sandwich with cranberry sauce!"
cried Runt. "Hooray!"

But no one ever listened to Runt.

It was Thanksgiving morning. Turk's family heard the *putt-putt-putt* of a little old car. Out of the car climbed a little old lady.

Wishbone Farm

"Maybe she's a little old talent scout," said Father.

"Maybe she's a little old dance instructor," said Mother.

"I hope she's a little old vegetarian," said Runt.

Father and Mother pushed Turk to the front of the barnyard.

"Show her what you've got!"

But before Turk could perform even one pirouette,

the little old lady scooted him aside.

"Aha!" she exclaimed, pointing at Runt.

"Exactly what I've been looking for.

This bird is the just the right size for me."

"What!?" cried Mother.

"Him!?" cried Father.

"Help!" cried Runt.

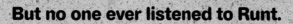

But no one ever listened to Runt.

So he ran.

He ran behind Father. "Don't let her eat me!"

He ran behind Mother. "Hide me! Hide me!"

He ran behind Turk. "I'm too young to be basted!"
Turk saw the look in the little old lady's eyes. He saw the drool on her lips.
He saw the fork in the little old lady's pocket. He saw the roasting pan
in her backseat! Runt had been right all along!

"Work with me, Runt!" Turk instructed. "Or your goose is cooked!"

Turk bobbed and weaved.

Runt flapped and drooled.

Turk leaped and twirled.

Runt coughed and wheezed.

Runt gobbled like a maniac while Turk dived down and tackled the little old lady's shoes.

"Stuff and nonsense!" cried the little old lady, climbing back into her car.

"I wouldn't eat these birds if they were the last turkeys on Earth."

That day, as the family feasted on corn and alfalfa,

they had much to be thankful for.

"I'm thankful we're all together," said Mother.

"I'm thankful for two brave sons," said Father.

"I'm thankful for such a smart brother," said Turk.

"We're not out of the woods yet," Runt warned. "Come December, folks begin planning their holiday dinners."

"Dinners that include stuffing?" asked Mother.
"Dinners that include gravy?" asked Father.

"Dinners that include m-m-me?" asked Turk.

"Over my feathered body!" Runt said.
"We're not plucked yet. I have a grade-A plan!"

And this time, *everyone* listened to Runt.